The Bandu Club

CARLA CAMPBELL

ILLUSTRATED BY RYAN HUMMER

Design: Baily Crawford

First Published: 2021

ISBN: 978-90-9034448-5

Iris and Norman, this is for you

I have learned that friendship isn't about who you've known the longest. It's about who came and never left your side.

Benson

Saved by the dinner bell

Benson sits down on his bed and reaches over to the scissors which are patiently waiting on his desk. He picks up Max, caresses him softly, and closes his eyes. The palms of his hands are clammy causing the scissors to slip around between his fingers.

Benson opens his eyes and looks out of the window. It's windy outside; the trees are swaying and the clothes that are drying on the line are whistling around like balloons. In the corner of his eye, he catches sight of a squirrel scrambling up a tree in his neighbour's garden. He watches as the squirrel finds an acorn and tries to open it. Benson is stalling. He wishes he had an excuse to stop but he knows in his heart this is the right time. *Focus!* he thinks. He takes another look at dear old Max and slowly opens the scissors. The blades are spread apart wide like a shark about to swallow a fish. He brings Max closer to the blades...hands trembling...sweating...

"Benson!" He freezes and sits still.

"Dinner's ready, come and get it!" his dad calls. Even though he has no appetite, Benson has one thought...*phew, saved by the dinner bell!*

This is Benson

Benson Williams is ten years old. His birthday is on the 14th of June, making him a Gemini. His Aunt Patricia had told him that Geminis are curious, kind, sociable, and energetic. Ever since, he's been trying to figure out if he possesses these qualities. Benson can lack confidence at times and has recently been striving not to over-think, and just go for it. He is tall for his age, with chocolate brown skin and short black, afro hair.

When he's older, Benson wants to get his hair styled in cornrows...just like the cool rappers!

He lives with his mum, dad, and sister Bianca. Bianca is six years old and Benson generally finds her annoying. Although recently they have enjoyed building Lego skyscrapers together, which is progress. The Williams family live in a three-bedroomed, semi-detached house in the town of Mable. Benson's favourite part of their home is the garden where he has a basketball net. He shoots balls whilst dreaming of becoming a professional basketball player. He figures that if he practises 'nearly every day' then eventually he'll make it onto the Los Angeles Lakers team.

His parents are Jamaican, and his Uncle Carson still lives on the island. Benson had visited Jamaica with his parents when he was two years old, but he can't remember anything about that trip.

"Do you remember that wonderful boat trip we took?" asked his mum.

Benson shook his head.

"How about riding in Uncle Carson's jeep to the market?"

"Nope" replied Benson.

His parents have promised to take the family soon. He dreams of traveling abroad to visit many countries, but in the meantime, he looks up places on Google to satisfy his curiosity.

Benson's family loves to gather together, and they don't need a reason or purpose for doing so. They get together, share large meals, and converse over the dinner table. Soulful music blares as they fill their plates with ackee and saltfish; fried plantain and curried goat. Benson loves these get-togethers...although it's during one of these gatherings that his family discover his secret. A memory that Benson would rather forget...

I wish the ground would swallow me up

Benson reaches over the table and ladles rice and peas onto his plate. He's trying to leave enough room for banana pancakes, which his Aunt Patricia expertly cooks. He's happy right now, what more could he ask for? Family, food, music in his home; the perfect combination. He's over the moon that his cousins Lloyd and Junior have come along.

"Hey man, so good to see you!" Junior fist pumps Benson. "This food smells amazing!" he says, wandering off to investigate.

Benson sits down on a chair, savouring every mouthful of food as he watches his joyful family. Suddenly, timed with a pause in the music, Lloyd swings open the door bursting into the dining room. He is bent over laughing. Everyone stops eating to look at him, Benson does too. He rests his fork on the plate that teeters on his lap. His laughing is contagious that one by one the family starts laughing with him before knowing why.

“Hey Lloyd, what’s so funny?” asks Aunt Patricia.

Lloyd doesn’t hear as the noise in the room is increasing in volume.

“Lloyd, care to share?” asks Junior.

Lloyd composes himself and stands up straight. He digs around in the back pocket of his jeans and pulls out a rag, dangling it up high so everyone can see. Benson holds his breath, the blood draining away from his face, *I wish the ground would swallow me up!* he thinks.

“What is that?” asks Junior.

“It looks like you’ve cleaned my car with that!” laughs Aunt Patricia.

Lloyd spins around to face Benson, “This, I believe, belongs to you!”

Benson feels all eyes on him. His mind is racing...*should I deny all knowledge or should I just come clean?* Before he has a chance to decide, Bianca runs into the room to find out what all the commotion is about.

"Oh, that's Max, Benson's blanket. Lloyd found it in the bathroom and asked me what it is," she says. No secret is safe with her!

Everyone roars with laughter and Uncle John pads over to squeeze Benson's cheek, "Coochy-coochy-coo!" he says.

Lloyd is still waving Max around when Benson feels a sudden surge of anger rise from within his body. He jumps up, his plate falls onto the carpet, rice and peas splatter into a colourful mess. His hands form fists, and he squeezes tight enough for all of his knuckles to go white. He reaches out to grab Max from Lloyd, who jerks Max just out of his grasp. In seconds, Benson is chasing Lloyd around the dining table, hitting pots of food and knocking plates to the ground as they go. Chink! Chink! Splat!

"Boys, if you want to play chase you'd better go to the garden," says Uncle John.

With that, the two of them run outside, cooling off with Junior. Before long they are shooting balls in the basket. Benson is relieved for a change of subject.

That evening whilst waving goodbye to the last of their family, his mum turns to him,

"I'm pretty sure they'll all forget about Max," she says.

Benson doesn't respond and he wanders into the kitchen; as he passes the fridge something catches his eye. Hanging on the door attached with a magnet, Max is on full display beside the words, *'MAX WAS HERE'*. Clearly, his family refuse to forget!

The story of Max

When Benson was born his parents received lots of visits from friends and family. A lady named Fern, who lived on the same street, came around one Saturday afternoon to meet him.

“Ahh, isn’t he a bonny baby,” she said. “Can I hold him?”

His mother nodded and gently handed her bundle of joy over to the woman. Fern held Benson in her arms and gazed adoringly into his rich brown eyes. She continued to hold him whilst she nattered to his parents about the gossip from the street.

“You’ll never guess what I found out. Reggie at number 37 just bought a new car, a Porsche to be exact. I just don’t know where he gets his money from, he only works in the butchers,” she muttered.

Fern passed Benson back to his mum and started digging around in her large handbag.

“I nearly forgot! Here’s a little something for Benson,” she exclaimed, handing his father a gift, wrapped in yellow tissue paper. He unwrapped the paper and found a very soft blanket covered in teddy bears.

“Oh, how lovely, thank you,” said Benson’s mum.

After finally waving goodbye to Fern they put Benson to bed, swaddling him in the blanket. As Benson grew older, he developed a fondness for the blanket. Wherever Benson crawled to, the blanket followed in tow. When Benson began to walk, he would hold it in his chubby hand and took it everywhere.

One day when Benson was three years old, his dad took a long look at him.

“Well Benson, does your blanket have a name?”

Benson thought this was a brilliant idea. *Why in his three years on earth had he not thought of this?* He looked around the room for inspiration. He had watched a cartoon earlier with a dog named Max. He looked at his blanket and then turned his gaze to his dad.

"My blanket is called Max," he proudly announced.

By the time Benson was six years old, he'd noticed that children his age didn't carry around keepsakes such as his blanket, so he made an executive decision that Max would remain in his bed. He was sad that he could no longer take him out and about, but he was comforted by the fact that Max was waiting for him every time he went to bed. He couldn't sleep without Max, let alone imagine life without him.

Whenever he saw Fern pottering about in her garden, he always gave her a big smile and a wave. He was forever grateful that she had come around that Saturday afternoon with a present that he would never forget!

The idea

The teasing Benson received from his family was the trigger to cut up Max. Since the day he was saved by the dinner bell, he hadn't tried again. Benson has decided to forget about this episode, instead concentrating his mind on his friends.

His group of friends makes up the Bandu Club. The name was created by bundling the first letter of each member's name. B is obviously for Benson; A is for Amy; N is for Nelly; D is for Dana and U is for UJ. They all met at a youth club three years ago and now call each other best friends. Even though it seems like a lifetime ago that they met each other, they continue to grow closer with time.

They don't all go to the same school, but they do have a pact to meet up once a week. Benson is excited as their next meet up is tomorrow at Amy's. He arrives at school that day with a big grin on his face. He bumps into the only one of the Bandu Club who goes to his school, Dana, during break time.

"Hey," she says. "Have you got your idea ready for the meet up?"

Benson looks blankly at her. *What is she talking about?*

Dana laughs, "You've forgotten, haven't you?"

"Er, yes!"

"We're going to share ideas for our next adventure."

"Right," he says. "I've got this. I'll bring the best idea to Amy's."

Dana's eyes twinkle, "Oh yeah, you haven't heard my idea yet!"

With that, she confidently skips down the corridor to her classroom. Benson can't wait for this school day to finish so that he can rush home to get his ideas ready.

***

Benson closes the front door behind him.

"Hi Mum!" he shouts.

His mum pops her head out of the kitchen, but he has already shot up the stairs. “Kids!” she says.

Benson flings back his duvet, finds Max, and sits crossed-legged on his bed snuggling him. *Quick!* He gets out his huge drawing book and starts scribbling down ideas.

Build a fully functioning robot? Nope...too tricky!

Learn to sail a boat? Nobody has a boat!

Eventually, he comes up with his best idea yet. He creates a mind map on the paper and cannot wait to show his friends!

The meet up

The Bandu Club loves going to Amy's home as the snacks are always delicious...spring rolls, dumplings, bao's with gooey fillings, and sweet steamed cake are some of their favourites.

Once everyone has arrived, Amy's mum carries plates of dumplings and crispy egg rolls into the lounge. UJ takes a bite of an egg roll, "Oh yeah, that's what I'm talking about!"

The conversation is always free-flowing between the Bandu Club. As they natter about school, Dana interrupts, "Ok everyone, shall we share our adventure ideas?"

Everyone stops and smiles. No words are needed to show their agreement.

"Who's going first?" she asks.

"I will," says Nelly.

Nelly's idea – clear her garage at home and make a den

UJ's idea – overnight camping trip with his dad

Amy's idea – cooking lesson with her mum to make Chinese snacks

Dana's idea – a trip to the Mega theme park (she wants to ride the new rollercoaster!)

"Benson, ready to share your amazing idea?" asks Dana.

Benson digs around in his rucksack and pulls out his mind map. He unfolds it, spreading it out on the low coffee table. He takes a nervous deep breath before speaking.

"I think we should form a basketball team," he says, pointing to the centre of his mind map. "A basketball team needs five people and guess what, there are five of us! I figured we could ask a few kids at our schools to be the subs, then we could join a basketball league."

He traces his finger down a line to a red circle, 'League Champions'. He has drawn a trophy next to the words for added effect. Benson's heart is racing with excitement, but as he looks up, he sees four bewildered faces looking at him.

"I don't think I'm tall enough to be a basketball player," says Amy.

There's a short silence, broken by Dana, "Ok, let's vote!"

She hands everyone a pencil and a strip of paper.

"Write down your favourite adventure. One rule, you can't vote for your own."

Benson quickly considers which adventure he would prefer. Even though his friends went suspiciously quiet after his presentation, he's still hopeful that he can win some votes. He decides that the trip to the theme park will be the most fun.

Dana reads out the results, "Amy's cooking lesson has one vote and my theme park idea has one vote. With three votes...the winner is.... UJ's camping trip!"

UJ jumps up cheering, "Oh man, it's going to be so much fun. My dad has the best tent, it's huge!"

Everyone congratulates UJ and they agree it will be the best adventure yet. Everyone apart from Benson. His ears are ringing as he stares forward and all he can think about is camping without Max. He can't even sleep without Max!

Dad to the rescue

Benson is busily opening his drawers to see what he should pack for the camping trip. His rucksack has two pairs of trousers and some socks in it. He grabs his baseball cap and puts it in. He found a plastic bag in the kitchen which is going to hide Max at the bottom of his rucksack. "Genius idea!" he mutters to himself.

Just as he is stuffing Max in, his dad comes into his bedroom.

"Hey, my son, how's the packing going?"

"Ok," shrugs Benson.

"I used to be an avid camper when I was younger. Come on, let me check you have everything you need."

Before Benson can reply his dad has turned his rucksack upside down and all the contents fall out. It doesn't look like much on the bed as his dad sifts through it.

"Two pairs of trousers, socks, and a baseball cap, that's all you think you need?"

His dad flings open his wardrobe and gathers more socks, some boxer shorts, two t-shirts, and a jumper.

"There, that's more like it. You'll also need a waterproof jacket."

He is actually glad of his dad's help, as he doesn't want to be the least prepared member of the Bandu Club. His dad eyes the plastic bag as he helps repack the rucksack.

"What's in here then?" he looks inquisitively at Benson.

"Erm, nothing, just thought I'd bring a plastic bag in case of an emergency."

His dad shakes Max out of the bag. Benson looks down at the floor, embarrassed and disappointed in himself for lying.

“Hey, it’s ok to take Max with you. I’m pretty sure everyone has their own little quirks,” his dad says, sitting on the bed.

“What does that mean?”

“When I was younger I had a toy rabbit that I took everywhere. Sure enough, I was teased by my big brother. Then one day when I was rooting through his bedroom looking for something, I discovered that he had a blanket under his pillow. It made me realise that everyone has some sort of comforter that they turn to. I’m talking about your Uncle John. Can you imagine big old Uncle John with a cuddly blanket?” he chuckles.

A smile spreads across Benson’s face. He feels a little better but he’s still worried that his friends will find out. *What would they say? How would they react?*

Just then Bianca comes bounding through his bedroom door.

"I wish I could come," she sighs.

"When you're older you can go camping. That reminds me, I have a few things for you in the shed," and off his dad goes.

"What do you do in the Bandu Club?" asks Bianca.

"Well, we find out where haunted houses are and we go looking for ghosts," says Benson.

"Really?" says Bianca, jumping back.

"As if! We just have lots of fun together. I guess you could say we are best friends."

"Are there rules for your club?"

"No there aren't actually."

He thinks that this could be a good idea. *Perhaps Bianca isn't so annoying after all?* As he drifts into a daydream about making a 'rules list', his dad comes in with his arms full.

"You'll need these," he says, carefully placing a water bottle, toilet roll, torch, and compass on the bed.

"What's all of this?" Bianca asks.

"These my dear are camping essentials."

Benson's pretty sure he won't need most of his father's additions but packs them up anyway. Just then, they hear the beep of a car horn. Bianca looks out of the window.

"It's the Bandu Club!"

Benson throws his rucksack on his back and the three of them run downstairs. He grabs his waterproof jacket, gives each of his family members a hug, and opens the door to see the smiling faces of the Bandu Club. UJ's dad is in the driver's seat and he's singing along to the radio. *This is going to be a real adventure!*

The misadventure

UJ's dad parks the car and all the kids jump out.

"Woah! The trees are so tall!" says Benson. They all look up at them.

"I feel dizzy," says Nelly.

"Ok campers, let's go and find a spot to put up our tent," says UJ's dad.

They walk for about fifteen minutes until they come across an opening in the trees, leading to a section of grass near a sparkling, blue river.

"This is so beautiful," says Amy.

"Isn't it? I used to camp here with my family when I was a boy. This area's called Drakewood," says UJ's dad.

Benson digs around in his pocket and pulls out the compass. He places it in the palm of his hand and the arrow hovers around North. He looks up, making sure that no one is paying any attention to what he's doing. Feeling relieved, he's pretty sure he can sneak in Max without anyone noticing. UJ's dad starts pulling out the tent from its bag.

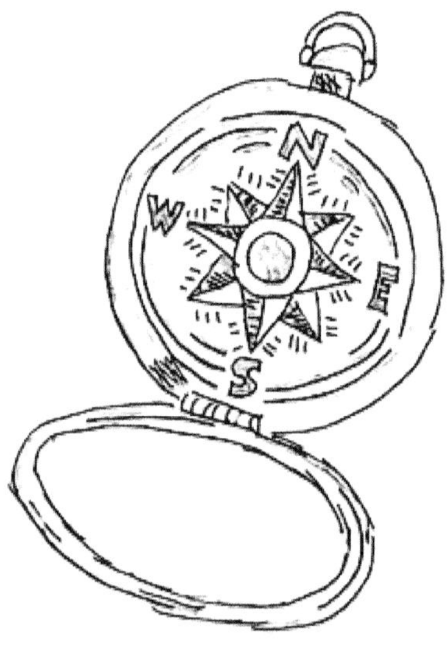

"So, I would like two of you to help me put up the tent while the other three look for firewood," he says.

It's decided that UJ and Amy will help with the tent whilst Benson, Nelly, and Dana go into the forest.

“Only take wood that is already on the ground and don’t go too far,” says UJ’s dad.

“Ok!” shouts back Dana.

The three of them walk through the forest, admiring their surroundings. They see wildflowers in every shade of colour and birds flying around in the trees. They pick up branches, placing them in the bag that Nelly is carrying.

“We have two big bags so let’s try and fill them up,” says Dana.

Wandering left, wandering right, they come across a swing hanging between two sturdy trees. They each have a turn pushing and swinging, urging each other to go higher. Nelly begins to feel cold and suggests they head back to the camp as the two bags of wood are full.

“Ok, which way?” asks Dana.

The three of them stand together, then slowly turn around to see if they can figure out the direction to the camp. Nelly starts shivering.

"Oh no, I think we're lost. The forest all looks the same to me!"

Dana, who's feeling more confident, takes charge.

"Right, I think we go that way," she points firmly with her finger and starts marching in that direction. Nelly doesn't move and is about to let the tears flow when Benson suddenly has a thought.

"Wait!" he shouts to Dana, who promptly stops, swinging around to look at them.

"I have a compass," he says.

"A what?" asks Dana, who starts walking back to them.

Benson places the compass in his hand and they all look down at it.

"I tested it out earlier at camp and the arrow was facing North, which must mean we go that way?"

Dana is disappointed that she hasn't come up with a bright idea.

"I think we use the compass to get us back," says Benson.

He starts walking towards the direction that the compass designated as North. The three of them slowly trudge back through the forest and this time it's a little darker, a little spookier. There are unfamiliar noises and eerie shadows. After a lot of trudging, they eventually come across the opening. Benson breathes a sigh of relief, feeling the weight of the responsibility to get the group back to camp safely lift off his shoulders.

"They're back!" shouts Amy when she catches sight of Benson.

"Thank goodness!" says UJ's dad, "We were about to send out a search party for you."

Nelly runs past Benson and throws her arms around Amy.

"We got lost but Benson saved the day with his compass. I really thought we were going to be eaten by wolves!" she says.

"Wow, did you see wolves?" asks UJ.

"Err, no. But I'm sure they would have found us...eventually," says Nelly.

"Hey, well done Benson. A good camper never leaves home without a compass," says UJ's dad.

He sounds just like my dad! thinks Benson. He smiles and wanders into the freshly put up tent for some quiet time. He chooses a sleeping bag, pulls Max from his rucksack, and lays down cuddling him. Benson is overcome with tiredness and closes his eyes. He has been dozing for a few minutes when he feels a presence. Slowly opening his eyes he sees the Bandu Club flitting between staring at him and staring at Max. Benson sits up abruptly.

"I can explain!" he says.

"What is it?" asks Dana.

"Erm...erm...it's my comfort blanket."

"Aren't you too old for that?" she asks.

"I guess I am," says Benson, feeling embarrassed.

"I think it's special," says Amy, keen to change the atmosphere in the tent.

"Thanks, Amy. My family teased me about it which makes me feel silly, I guess," says Benson.

"Yeah, sorry, it's just I've never seen one before," replies Dana. She leans over and hugs Benson. UJ is speechless for once and is not sure what to say to Benson.

"Oh, ignore your family, I have a baby grow that I like to cuddle when I'm sad or scared. I sure could have used it in the forest back then!" says Nelly.

"Oh right, when all the wolves were chasing you?" says UJ.

Nelly picks up a pillow and bounces it on UJ's head. He grabs another pillow and bounces it back. Dana finds a pillow and swings it at

Benson's legs. He jumps up and grabs his own one. Before long all of the Bandu Club are involved in a pillow fight to beat all pillow fights! Benson hasn't laughed this much in ages. UJ's dad pokes his head in the tent, laughing as he sees the carnage.

"Sorry to break up the fun but dinner's ready!"

They all clamber out to find a fire with eggs and beans cooking over it in a skillet.

"You're the best!" Amy tells UJ's dad and they all cheer.

After dinner everyone is relaxed; UJ's dad gets out his guitar and starts playing songs. Whilst the others try to learn the words, UJ comes and sits next to Benson who is keeping warm by the fire.

"I hope we didn't ruin your quiet time earlier," says UJ.

"No, it was ok," says Benson.

"How long have you had your blanket?"

Benson hesitates to answer, worried that his friend will laugh. He steals a glance at UJ's face and decides to push his fear down.

"Since I was a baby. I used to drag it around everywhere but now I just sleep with it."

"Does the blanket make you feel better?"

Benson gives it a few moments of thought.

"It does actually. It makes me feel safe. Guess it's not really cool though," says Benson.

UJ laughs, "Cool is what you make it. I'll tell you what I think is cool though, learning to play the guitar. Come on," he says, and they head over to the wannabe singers.

Parting ways

Benson returns home from the camping trip full of confidence. After the conversations with his friends, he had pushed Max to the bottom of his rucksack. Sleeping next to his friends that night was enough to comfort him. He had missed out on sleepovers before and now it's time to part ways.

"Mum, can you come up to my room please?" he shouts downstairs.

His mum climbs the stairs and enters his room. "What can I do for you?" she asks.

"Can you hold Max please?"

She does so and watches as Benson opens a drawer and pulls out the scissors.

"Are you sure? You don't have to."

Benson is adamant and opens up the scissors.

His mum holds up a hand, "Why don't we just tuck Max away in your memory box in the attic?"

Benson pauses and thinks about this suggestion. *Maybe I don't have to cut him up to move on?* he thinks.

"Sure," he says, giving Max one last caress. "Goodbye Max."

His mum pulls him towards her for a hug.

Just then they hear Bianca's voice, "Lloyd and Junior are here!" she calls up.

Benson smiles at his mum and runs downstairs. His two cousins are already shooting balls into the basket.

“Hey, what’s up?” asks Benson.

“You’re in a good mood,” says Junior.

“Just had a cuddle with Max?” laughs Lloyd, who aims the ball at the net. It misses!

“Who’s Max?” says Benson, taking his own shot and watching it swish straight through the net. He smiles, running to pick up his ball.

Amy

The awakening

"Amy, it's time to wake up!" shouts Mae through the gap in her bedroom door. Amy groans, rolls over, and pulls the duvet over her head. She's tired this morning and her body needs more time in bed. She's just about to fall back to sleep when she realises what day it is. *My swimming lesson is today!*

"Eurgghhh!" she groans.

Amy doesn't like swimming. Fact.

She gets out of bed and creeps along the corridor to find her mum who is setting up the table for breakfast.

“I don’t feel so well,” she croaks.

“Why, what’s wrong?” asks her mum.

“I have a sore throat and a headache.”

“Open your mouth.”

Amy does what she is told and her mum shines the light from her phone into her mouth.

“There’s nothing wrong with you, now go and get changed,” she snaps.

Amy rolls her eyes and slowly saunters back to her bedroom. Although the weather is mild, Amy pulls on a long-sleeved top, followed by a jumper and of course, her beloved jeans. She delves around in her wardrobe and pulls out her swimming bag. She hurries back to her mum and asks her to put her silky black hair into bunches. It’s part of their daily ritual, and how she always wears her hair—even on swimming lesson day.

Her family sits down for a breakfast of congee and dough sticks. Mae arrives, the sounds of faint beeps fill the air.

“No phones at the dining table!” says Amy. Mae gives her a glare.

“The best breakfast in the world!” says her dad.

This is Amy

Amy Chan is ten and a half years old and she never lets anyone forget the half! Her birthday is on the 4th of March—which she likes as flowers are blooming and animals are being born. Amy is an exceptional artist and her birthday month inspires her to paint, draw, and create art related to nature. She has mid-length black hair and dark eyes to match.

She lives in a third-floor apartment in the town of Mable with her mum, dad, and sister Mae. The rest of her family likes to take the lift, whereas Amy prefers to run up the stairs! Her sister Mae is fourteen years old, making her a 'teenager'. She has recently noticed that Mae has started to wear make-up, listen to lots of music in her room (with the door closed!), and is texting boys. Amy thinks this is weird and can't ever imagine being like that.

Her parents are Chinese and moved away from China before the two of them were born, seeking better fortunes in the western world. They run a printing business, making anything from invitations to promotional leaflets. Occasionally they ask the girls to help out in the shop, and although Mae moans, Amy always enjoys it as she can be creative with her designs. In fact, Amy's biggest strength is her willingness to help.

The Chan family only has a few relatives who live nearby, so her mum spends lots of time on the phone speaking Mandarin to their friends and family. Amy can speak Mandarin but she prefers speaking English at home.

Amy loves being part of the Bandu Club and even though her mum says they are too noisy when they come over, Amy knows she likes them all...especially when they gush over her homemade food! Amy is particularly excited as the next meet up is at Nelly's house and they are going to have an art class...with Amy as the teacher! The meet up is in two days' time, but before that, she needs to get through her swimming lesson...

The swimming lesson

Amy is in the same class as Nelly at school. They both wish that the other Bandu Club members went to the same school, but they make do with a nice bunch of kids from their class. Amy and Nelly mostly hang out with Molly and Sienna.

"I love swimming, it's the best part of the week," says Sienna, as they are finishing off their school assignment.

"Yeah, so much fun!" says Nelly. Molly nods in agreement.

"How about you Amy, do you like swimming?" asks Sienna.

Amy pretends that she hasn't heard and continues to look engrossed in her sums.

“Amy?” says Sienna.

“Oh yeah...I guess swimming is OK,” she responds.

The bell rings, their teacher tells them to pack up and get their swimming bags. It’s a short walk to the pool. The female changing area is a big open room and this bothers Amy. She chooses her spot in the corner with the hope that fewer kids will see her. She whips off her clothes, keeping on her long-sleeved top until last. She feels anxious and is trying to keep calm. Having put on her swimming shorts, she exchanges her top for a long-sleeved swimming top. She doesn't speak to anyone in the changing room and is relieved that the rest of the girls chat and mess around leaving her be. She walks through the open doors to the pool, sits down on the bench, and takes a deep breath. Five minutes pass before all of the children are ready. A kid named Billy leans over and looks at her for a moment,

"Why do you have a long-sleeved top on?" he asks.

Amy feels herself blushing and she quickly thinks of a response. Avoiding any eye contact she replies, "The sleeves keep me warm in the water."

"Oh right," says Billy unconvincingly. He swings back to face his friends on the bench.

Amy knows she looks different from the other children during swimming lessons. They all wear trunks or swimsuits that show most of their skin. Deep in thought, she misses the instructions from the teacher and notices that she is the only one left on her bench. She quickly stands up and jumps in the pool.

Artists in the making

Amy perks herself up with the thought of the next Bandu Club meeting and before she knows it, the day has arrived. She has packed up all of her art supplies and her mum has kindly bought enough easels and blank canvases for the group. Amy is excited at the prospect of teaching her friends about painting and sharing her skills. Her grandmother was an artist and a few years ago in China, she had taught Amy everything from the different brush strokes; types of paint and styles; to blending colours. Amy treasures her special memories of her grandmother, who has since passed away. She feels that it's her responsibility to keep up the love of art in the Chan family in her absence. Mae is only interested in boys and her parents don't have much time for it.

With school finished and some dumplings warming her tummy, she is ready to rock. She arrives at Nelly's house early so she can set up her materials. Nelly takes her up to the attic room which is warm and cosy with its slanted roof. The leather sofas have been pushed back to make room to set up the easels.

UJ arrives next, followed by Benson and Dana.

"I'm so excited about your art class Amy!" squeals Dana.

"Yeah, my dad said I need to take my mind off sports for once and concentrate on the arts," says UJ.

"Can I paint my favourite basketball team?" asks Benson.

Amy looks at him, rolling her eyes. Nelly's mum has laid out snacks for them, a huge bowl of Cheetos and orange juice. Once they have finished eating, Amy clears her throat to speak.

"Ok everyone, I hope you are all ready for an art masterclass," she says with a grin.

The Bandu Club erupts in cheering and clapping!

"You each have an easel, canvas, a selection of paintbrushes, a pot of water, and a paint palette," she informs them.

"What's a palette?" asks UJ.

She lifts one up and explains that each section of the palette holds a different coloured paint.

"Please choose an easel and stand in front of it," she says.

She walks over to the coffee table in the middle of the room. There is an object covered in a tea towel on the table and slowly she pulls it off to reveal a big bowl of ripe fruit.

“Wow!” says Benson.

“That looks delicious!” says Dana.

“You can eat it after you have painted it,” chuckles Amy.

“I’m up for the challenge!” says UJ.

They get to work and Amy paces around the room, explaining that they are about to learn what is called still life painting. She informs them about shading, mixing colours, and creating shadows. They have been painting for a while when UJ mentions, "My water's dirty, shall I change it?" he asks.

"Sure," says Amy.

UJ walks across the room to the sink. He changes the water and starts walking back to his easel. He is so busy trying not to spill the water that he doesn't see the edge of the coffee table and he trips. His arms stretch out clutching the water pot, but his feet are unable to balance him. He staggers forward and the water goes all over Amy, who is standing next to his easel.

"Owww!" she shouts, "That water's hot!"

Without hesitation, Amy pulls off her wet top and flings it on the floor. Dana gasps. The rest of the Bandu Club stop what they are doing and are now looking at Amy. She is damp and has tears forming, teetering on the brims of her eyes. Feeling exposed with her top off in front of everyone, she knows what they are looking at. She sobs, runs towards the door, down the attic stairs, and locks herself in the bathroom.

That's what friends are for

UJ is pale and places the pot on the table. "I didn't realise the water was hot," he says.

"Which tap did you use? asks Nelly.

UJ looks over to the sink, "The left one," he replies.

Nelly places her hand on her forehead, "That's the hot water tap."

"I don't think the water burned Amy, I just think she got a shock," says Benson reassuringly.

Dana pulls herself together, "We need to go and see if Amy is ok."

Nelly volunteers to check on Amy and thinks it would be best if UJ came along too. She gently taps on the bathroom door.

"Amy, it's me, Nelly. Are you ok?"

The pair of them wait for a few seconds but Amy doesn't respond.

"Hey Amy, I'm really sorry about what happened. Do you think we could come in?" asks UJ.

They wait again, then hear the lock slowly turning. Nelly pushes down the handle, opens the door and they see Amy sitting on the bathroom floor wrapped in a towel. They sit down next to her and Nelly wraps her into a big hug.

"I'm so sorry," says UJ.

"It's ok," says Amy. "I guess I always knew that I couldn't hide it forever."

She slowly drops the towel from her shoulders and they can now see her arms, which are covered in red, scaly patches.

"It's called psoriasis," Amy tells them. "It can be itchy but you can't catch it. I've had it since I was little and I have always tried to cover it up. It's on my back too."

Nelly thinks about the swimming lessons and it now makes sense why Amy wears a long-sleeved swimming top.

"Is there any medicine that you can take for it?" asks UJ.

"Not really, I have some cream that I use. Oh, and the sunlight is good for it."

"It doesn't make you any less beautiful," says Nelly, giving Amy another squeeze.

"Thanks, guys. I guess I feel better now that you know. It's really hard trying to cover it up all the time. I'm always worried about what other people will think."

"Don't worry about other people. I bet most people wouldn't even notice it. Now it makes sense why you always wear long sleeve tops no matter what the weather is like," says UJ, who rubs Amy's shoulder and gives her his biggest smile.

"Come on, let's go and have a look at everyone's masterpieces," he suggests.

Nelly grabs a clean top from her bedroom and the three of them go back up the stairs to the attic where the other two are waiting. Dana and Benson both give Amy a hug and sit down to hear her explain her psoriasis. After everyone has given Amy their support, Benson tactfully changes the subject.

"Ok then, let's look at our paintings," he suggests.

One by one, they show their paintings of the fruit bowl. UJ is last and he turns his painting around, “Ta-da!” he says.

The Bandu Club starts laughing and before long they are all rolling around on the floor clutching their tummies.

"Hey, what's so funny?" asks UJ, pretending to be hurt.

"It looks like a flying saucer with big yellow lights!" laughs Dana.

"Oh!" says UJ, turning the painting around so he can inspect it.

"That's the bunch of bananas!" he sniggers.

With that, he starts laughing and joins his friends on the floor.

Heart to heart

The weekend arrives, giving Amy time to think about what happened. She feels relieved that her best friends now know, and she is grateful for their supportive reaction. Her parents are out at the fish market, so it's just Amy and Mae at home. Amy wanders down the corridor to Mae's room, putting an ear to the closed door to listen. She can hear pop music playing and occasional giggles. Amy knocks on the door and opens it. Mae, who is sitting cross-legged on her bed, quickly puts her phone down and looks up at Amy. She smiles, "Hey, what's up?"

"Oh nothing, just wondered what you were doing."

"Amy Chloe Chan, I know you better than you think. Something is playing on your mind."

Amy saunters over to the bed and sits down.

"Well maybe," she says shyly.

"Ok, hit me with it."

Amy takes a deep breath. "Yesterday, I held an art class at Nelly's house with the Bandu Club. UJ spilt water on me and I took my top off, so they all saw my psoriasis."

"So, what were their reactions?"

"They were amazing. They told me I was still beautiful, and they think people wouldn't even notice it anyway," says Amy.

"You really have a great bunch of friends there Amy," says Mae. "Unfortunately, there are people who don't like it when someone is different. They can be cruel with their words and actions. You need to be strong and not worry about what those people think. Just remember what your family and friends think...and what you think. Being different is cool though, I love being the only Asian in my class. Who wants to be like everyone else when you can stand out and be different?" says Mae.

Amy loves how confident Mae is. She looks at her sister in awe and is quiet for a few moments. Mae holds Amy's hand, "So how are we going to tackle this?"

Amy has spent time in bed thinking about her plan of action. She delivers it to Mae, "I want to wear a swimsuit to my next lesson. I don't want to cover up anymore."

Mae is excited now and thinks this is an excellent idea.

"Well then let's do it. Have you got a swimsuit?" she asks.

"Er... no," replies Amy. She hasn't thought that far ahead.

Mae jumps off her bed and grabs her wallet. "Well, let's go and get one then!"

Amy feels so lucky to have a sister like Mae. As they walk towards the front door Mae stops and touches Amy's shoulder, "I'm so proud of you."

With that, they run out the front door and are ready to hit the shops.

Different is cool

Amy is nervous. It's swimming lesson day. She tells Nelly about her new suit, and her friend supports her decision to be brave. Amy chooses the same spot, as usual, to get changed, as she doesn't want to draw extra attention to herself. As she stands in her new, blue flowery swimsuit, she feels exposed, but at the same time exhilarated. *I can do this*, she thinks.

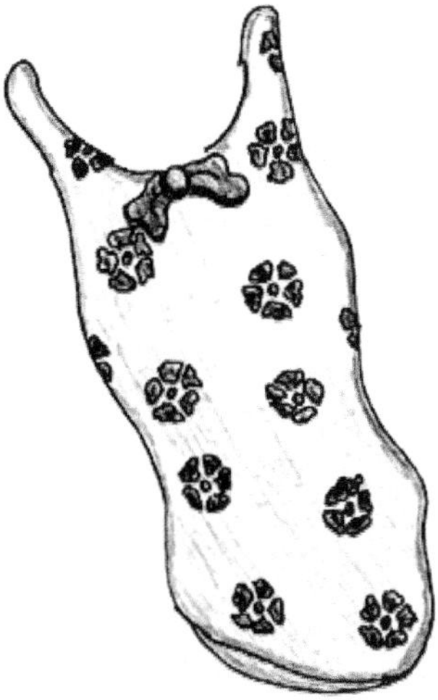

Molly and Sienna both notice her swimsuit and come closer to have a look. As they draw nearer, they both see Amy's red patches.

"Are you ok?" asks a concerned Sienna.

"Sure, I feel great," says Amy.

Nelly notices that Amy is flushed, so gives her a reassuring smile.

"I have psoriasis which causes my skin to be red and sometimes itchy. It's not contagious," Amy tells them.

"What does that mean?" asks a confused Molly.

"It means you can't catch it," replies Nelly.

"Oh right. My cousin has eczema and that's non-con-tag-ious too", says Molly.

"Your swimsuit is really nice," says Sienna, who links arms with her, and they trot out to the pool.

A boy named Tim starts sniggering and pointing at Amy as she walks past him. She can feel herself blushing and is worried that everyone is staring at her. She wants to run back into the changing room and hide, but then she remembers Mae's words, *"Who wants to be like everyone else when you can stand out and be different?"*

Billy, the kid who had previously asked her about her long-sleeved top, walks over to Tim. He bends over and says something in his ear. Tim turns pale and looks embarrassed. Billy then walks over to Amy.

"Your swimsuit looks way better than your long-sleeved top," says Billy.

"Oh...th...thanks," stumbles Amy.

Billy smiles and walks off. Sienna suddenly breathes out loudly, "He is so cute!" she says.

The four girls giggle, stand up and jump in the pool. Amy has the best lesson she has ever had!

Sunshine date

Nelly has remembered that sunshine is good for Amy's psoriasis so the next time she goes to her home, she speaks to Mae.

"Can we arrange a 'sunshine' date for Amy?" she asks.

Mae looked confused.

"Amy said that sunshine helps her psoriasis, so can you please help me look up the weather forecast? I would like to arrange a trip to the park with the Bandu Club," explains Nelly.

"Oh right, that's a great idea!" says Mae, reaching over for her phone. "Let's see. Ooh, this Saturday is warm and sunny."

"Great, would you like to come too? We probably need someone older to look out for us," asks Nelly.

"Sure, that would be fun."

That Saturday the Bandu Club have a picnic in the park. Amy wears a dress with short sleeves...she is proud to show off her arms. As they all relax on the rug after an energetic game of softball, Amy notices two figures heading their way. Mae notices too and quickly gets out her compact mirror to have a look at herself.

“You look beautiful,” mocks UJ.

“Oooh, Samuel’s coming our way!” says Benson.

Samuel is the boy who Mae texts! thinks Amy.

“It’s Billy too,” says Nelly excitedly.

“He’s Samuel’s brother,” says Mae.

“Hey guys, how are you all doing?” asks Samuel as they reach the group.

“We’re great!” says UJ.

Samuel sits next to Mae and she passes him some grapes. His brother takes a seat with the Bandu Club.

"We heard you had words with Tim," says Dana.

"News travels fast!" says Billy.

Dana laughs, "Well what did you say to him?"

All eyes are on Billy, they all want to know as badly as Dana.

"I told him that every time he laughs at somebody his nose will grow a little longer, until one day, it will be the length of a tennis racquet."

“Oh man, you didn’t?” says UJ with an open mouth.

“I like your style, but isn’t that a made-up story about Pinocchio?” asks Dana.

“Sure it is, but he believed me. You should have seen his face, it looked like he had seen a ghost!” laughs Billy.

The Bandu Club all look at Amy who is beaming. If she ever needs anyone to help her out again…she knows who to ask!

Nelly

Matthew

Nelly clicks in her seatbelt and her mum starts driving towards town. Every Tuesday after school Nelly sees Matthew. Nelly thinks he's old, but her mum assures her he's *"only in his late twenties." Maybe his beard makes him look older?* thinks Nelly. Regardless of what he looks like, Matthew makes Nelly feel confident, secure, and smart.

As they pull up outside Nelly grabs her special bag.

"Right, I'm going to browse around the shops whilst you're with Matthew. Try your best!" says her mum.

"I always do!" Nelly yells back.

She sits outside Matthew's room whilst he finishes a session with a boy.

"Hi Nelly!" he says, as he catches a glimpse of her, waving the boy off.

"Come on in," he says, beckoning her into his room.

They both sit down on the chairs of a round table.

"How was your weekend?" he asks.

Nelly tells him about her weekend in great detail: she made cupcakes with her mum; went to the cinema with her dad and brothers and had taken their dog Beanie for a walk in the park. She can talk for hours and even though Matthew loves listening to her stories, they have work to do.

Nelly finishes her session feeling great.

"How was it, love?" asks her mum as she climbs in the car.

"Really good thanks!"

"Glad to hear."

They pull out of the car park and head to their favourite Vietnamese restaurant to pick up dinner.

This is Nelly

What Nelly Riley likes most about herself is that people tell her she's caring. She loves animals, especially Beanie the pug, and is constantly pestering her parents for a cat. "You know what will happen, Nelly, we'll have a madhouse with Beanie chasing the cat all day!" her dad would say. Even though she is often told no on the subject, she has a feeling he will give in to her plea one day!

Nelly has long blonde hair, blue eyes and wears bright red glasses. She'll happily wear trousers one day, and a dress the next. She is eleven and a half years old and her birthday is on the 22nd of October. She's fully aware that she's older than the rest of the kids in her year group at school, as well as her friends in the Bandu Club. Most children don't notice this and she's hardly ever questioned about it.

Nelly has dyslexia and it was decided when she was seven years old that she would repeat a year at school, making her the oldest in her class. When Nelly started to learn the alphabet, she found it difficult to remember the names of them. She felt like her brain was scrambling up the information, making her development in reading and writing slower. With the help of her teachers and Matthew, she has made good progress over the last few years.

Nelly lives in a four-bedroomed detached house with her mum, dad, and two older brothers. Joe is fourteen and Zane is sixteen. They are both outstanding BMX riders and spend most of their free time competing at events. The Bandu Club, particularly Benson and UJ, think this is really cool! They live in Mable and always have. Her grandparents, great-grandparents, and even her great-great-grandparents lived in Mable. Zane always talks about moving abroad, which sends shivers down his parents' back!

As well as being the caring member of the family, she is also the ‘talker’. Nelly has started to call her friends for chats and her parents dread receiving the phone bill! They imagine it will only get worse as she gets older! Nelly’s amazing talking skills allow her to distract people from the fact that she has dyslexia.

Bandu Club rules

The next Bandu Club meeting is at Benson’s house and he has something *“pretty cool”* to share. Nelly hopes that it won’t be another suggestion to start a basketball team!

They all gather in the lounge of his house after school. Nelly looks around to see that his family is nowhere in sight. Benson’s mum and Bianca are at the library and his dad is working upstairs in the study. Benson's dad has left homemade carrot cake and iced lemonade on a small table for them to enjoy.

"Delicious!" says UJ stuffing the last piece of cake into his mouth.

"Right!" says Benson, "I think we should create a list of Bandu Club rules."

"Mmm," thinks Dana out loud, "What sort of rules?"

"Bianca asked me a while back if we have rules in the Bandu Club. I think it would be a good idea if we did," replies Benson.

In fact, he hasn't thought the plan through entirely and hopes that some other bright spark will provide inspiration.

"I think the rules should all be positive," suggests Nelly.

"Agreed!" says a delighted Benson, grabbing the pen and paper and giving it to Nelly. "How about you write down our suggestions?" he says to her.

Nelly feels a little uncomfortable with this task but is sure that all of Matthew's guidance will assist her in this time of need. Amy comes up with the first rule...*the Bandu Club are always there for each other*. Everyone thinks this is a brilliant first rule and Nelly starts to jot it down:

The Bando Club ar allways their for eash other

Amy notices that Nelly is blushing and quickly shows her how to correct the spelling. UJ who is now riding on a sugar high speaks up, "The second rule, the Bandu Club give compliments," he says.

"Cool!" nods Benson, relieved that his suggestion is going well.

The Bandu Club giv complyments

Quietly, Amy asks Nelly, “Would you like me to write the rules?”

“Sure,” says Nelly, handing over the pen and paper.

Matthew has taught Nelly to be confident about her dyslexia and he says it makes her special. However, she can sense that the others are feeling awkward and she doesn’t want this to continue.

“Is everything ok?” asks Amy, getting ready to write. Nelly takes in a deep breath and stands up.

“Ok guys,” she says and clears her throat, “I’m dyslexic and I’m finding it hard to spell correctly, so Amy is going to take over.” Nelly sits back down and waits for the flood of questions that are sure to follow.

“What’s dyslexic? UJ asks.

“Well, I’m dyslexic, but the condition is called dyslexia. It affects the area of my brain that processes language. So, I can find reading and writing more difficult as it takes a lot of time for me to sound out a word. That is why I repeated a year of school when I was seven, and why I'm older than all of you," she says.

"I always wondered why you were older than us," says UJ.

Dana gives him a look and mouths "compliment" to him.

"Oh right...erm...you're amazing Nelly!" he says in a fluster.

Dana grins, then reaches out to give Nelly a hug.

"You are brave for sharing this with us, Nelly. If there is anything we can do to make things easier for you, just let us know," she says.

"Agreed!" says Benson.

"Thanks," says Nelly.

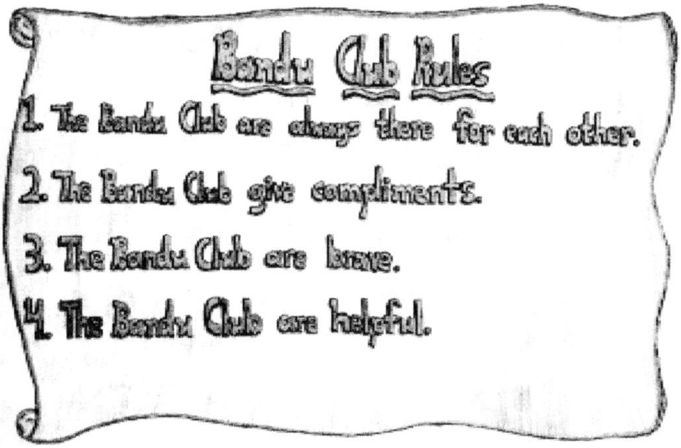

The conversation helps decide the next two Bandu Club rules – *The Bandu Club are brave,* and *The Bandu Club are helpful*. They agree that four rules are enough for the time being and to reward themselves they watch a classic film, Home Alone. They laugh together at the crazy haphazard burglars and Nelly feels a glow in her heart. She can't wait to tell Matthew!

Proud

Nelly has a hop in her step and literally skips into Matthew's room.

"Hey, you're in a good mood," says Matthew smiling.

"I am," says Nelly with an even wider grin than she walked in with.

"Did you win the lottery?"

"Not quite. I told my Bandu Club friends that I'm dyslexic."

Matthew is pleasantly surprised as Nelly has always kept her condition private.

"Good for you. So, how did it come about?" he asks.

"We were creating a list of rules for the club and I was picked to write them down. As you can imagine I didn't spell everything correctly. I didn't want my friends to feel sorry for me so I told them about my dyslexia."

"How did they react?"

"They had a few questions, but they were supportive. I feel like a weight has been lifted off my shoulders."

Matthew is beaming. "Nelly, you're amazing. Always remember that," he tells her.

They high-five and just like always get on with some work. Halfway through an activity, Nelly lifts her head and looks out of the window.

"Huh!" she gasps.

"Are you ok?" asks Matthew.

Standing outside the window are Benson and UJ kitted out in their taekwondo outfits, waiting to be picked up. As they laugh and chat, Nelly cautiously watches them when suddenly UJ looks into the window and catches her eye. He nudges Benson and they both look at her. Nelly can feel herself blushing.

"Are they part of your Bandu Club?" Matthew asks.

Nelly slowly nods. Matthew jumps up and leaves the room.

Where's he going? thinks Nelly. Before she knows it, UJ and Benson come bounding into the room. Matthew ushers them to sit down on a chair.

"Hey Nelly, Matthew said we could come in and say hi," says UJ.

"Hi," says Nelly shyly.

Matthew takes the lead and over the next ten minutes shows them what he and Nelly do during their sessions, and all the activities that help her feel more confident.

"If people are aware of what others are going through, then I believe it makes it easier for everyone," says Matthew.

"I agree," says UJ.

"Thanks for taking the time to explain. It's all much clearer now and I think you're so smart Nelly," says Benson, with UJ nodding in agreement.

The boys leave when they see UJ's dad park outside. There's a short silence in the room and Matthew silently wonders to himself whether or not he did the right thing. Nelly turns to him and for a second, her face is emotionless. Suddenly, a large grin forms on her face.

"Thanks!" she says.

That one word reassures him that he has.

Plant a tree

Nelly hears the letterbox and runs downstairs to check the post. She picks up a leaflet and slowly reads it:

Community project... Are you up for the challenge?

Help improve the environment by planting a tree.

Can you create the winning campaign?

Campaigns to be presented to the local council on the 1st of March.

Nelly is excited! *This could be a great project for the Bandu Club*, she thinks. Luckily there's a meet up at Dana's home tomorrow and she can't wait to show them all her idea.

***

Dana welcomes everyone into her home the next day, as they gather in her bedroom. Her mum brings up warm bread and dips to share. Dana has made a poster with the four Bandu Club rules and it looks great. After Amy tells them about her Chinese New Year, Nelly whips out the leaflet and they pass it around.

“Ooh, sounds fun!” says Dana.

“My mum phoned them to get more information. Basically, we can work as a team to come up with a campaign to encourage people to plant a tree. We will then present our ideas to the local council and whoever turns up on the day. The winning campaign will be provided with the young trees for people to plant,” explains Nelly.

“What’s a local council?” asks UJ.

“My mum says the local council is in charge of things like parks, housing, roads, and recycling. They also look after environmental health which is why they want people to start planting trees. So, who’s up for the challenge?” asks Nelly.

All their hands shoot up...the decision is unanimous! After much discussion, the Bandu Club decide that their campaign will be aimed at children.

“Ok, so we ask children to earn pocket money at home by doing something like washing the car or making lunch. Then, with this pocket money they buy a tree which they plant and can name whatever they want,” says Nelly.

“I would name my tree Coconut,” says UJ.

“Why would you choose that name?” asks Amy.

“In the hope that it would grow coconuts!” says UJ laughing.

Amy wonders what goes on in his head sometimes!

“Let’s have some thinking time and when we meet next week at UJ’s house we can plan some more. Cool?” asks Dana.

"Cool!" everyone replies.

They help tidy Dana's bedroom, and all leave feeling inspired and ready for this new challenge.

The campaign of the century!

Nelly longs for the week to pass so that the Bandu Club can be together again. She has spent some time with her brothers, Joe and Zane, preparing for the campaign. They are always encouraging towards Nelly and often help her with school projects.

"I like the idea of kids helping out and using the money to plant a tree," says Zane.

"Don't forget that they can then name their tree," says Nelly.

"Oh yeah, that's cool," chips in Joe. "I think you need a catchy slogan," he tells Nelly.

The three of them put their heads together and come up with 'Earn it, plant it, name it!' Nelly loves it and is grateful for the help of her brothers. Now she just hopes that the Bandu Club likes it as much as she does!

***

The weather is mild; they decide to sit around the table in UJ's garden. UJ loves hosting and he joins them with a bowl of nachos and salsa. Nelly feels confident and starts off by telling them about the importance of a slogan.

"Have you thought of one then?" asks Benson.

"Earn it, plant it, name it!" Nelly states proudly.

The Bandu Club falls silent for a few seconds, processing the new information. Nelly waits on bated breath.

"I love it!" says Dana.

"So do I!" says Amy.

Benson and UJ are grinning too, so it's agreed. The five of them get to work and share ideas. Dana explains that her dad knows the owner of an empty field and he's sure they will be interested in using it for the campaign. Amy takes control of the campaign poster and draws a hand holding a tree with the slogan surrounding it. Benson and UJ make a list of all of the jobs that children can do to earn money. Dana and Nelly prepare the tags which the children will use to name their trees.

UJ's mum brings them out some fruit and water. She scans over what they are up to, "It looks like the campaign of the century," she says cheekily. She winks at UJ and goes back into the house. Towards the end of the session they come up with some written prompts ready for their presentation next week, as it's agreed that they will all say a few words.

Nelly goes to bed that evening feeling confident and inspired. *Could they really have the campaign of the century?*

Earn it, plant it, name it!

It's the 1st of March—the day of the campaign presentation. The Bandu Club are heading into town with their families and have planned to meet next to the stage. Nelly is responsible for bringing the presentation cards, poster, list of jobs, and some examples of the name tags. She's silent in the car as she travels in with her mum, dad, Joe, and Zane.

As they park up, Joe leans over, whispering in her ear, "You'll do great today, I can feel it in my bones."

Nelly smiles at him and sees the other Bandu Club members waiting by the stage. As she walks up to them, she notices that UJ is looking pale and sad. His dad explains that he has woken up with a sore throat and has almost lost his voice. This doesn't deter the Bandu Club and it's agreed that Benson will say UJ's part of the presentation. UJ is happy enough just to hold up the poster.

After wishing them good luck, their families take their seats in front of the stage. The Bandu Club watch three other presentations before it's their turn. They wait by the steps leading up to the stage whilst the presenter introduces them.

"Ladies and gentlemen, we have our final campaign presentation now from a group called the Bandu Club. Please put your hands together," he says.

There is a round of applause and the Bandu Club scramble up the steps to the stage. As Benson takes the final step, he catches his shoe, stumbles forward, grabbing Amy's jumper. He pulls it so hard that they both tumble onto the floor, roll over a few times, and end up in a heap on the stage floor. The audience gasp! The presenter looks shocked, running over to check on them. Benson and Amy both look shaken up and Benson has a cut on his lip. They are helped down the steps by the presenter to sit and rest with their families. Disaster! *What are we going to do about Benson and Amy's speaking parts?* thinks Nelly.

This leaves three of the Bandu Club standing in a row on the stage: Nelly, Dana, and a non-speaking UJ. Nelly knows that it's now up to her and Dana to pull this off. Dana who is normally confident looks nervous. Nelly nods at her to start speaking.

"W...w...we are the Bandu Club and here is our campaign," says Dana slowly and quietly.

Nelly waits for her to continue speaking, but she doesn't. Dana's hands are trembling. Nelly feels the entire audience's eyes on her and raises her head to take a peep at them all. In the corner of her eye, she notices a familiar beard on a familiar face. *It is Matthew – he's in the audience!* She focuses on him and he slowly mouths,

"You can do it!"

Nelly takes a deep breath and looks down at the prompt cards in her hands. The words all seem to merge into one and it's just a blur to her. She quickly hands the prompt cards to Dana and starts to speak. She gains confidence as she explains the slogan, 'Earn it, plant it, name it!' and she shows the name tags. She refers to the poster that UJ is holding up and she even remembers to smile at the crowd! She ends the presentation on a positive note, "Any money which we make during our campaign will be put back into buying more trees. Trees are our future and the future is green!"

Nelly takes another deep breath, glad that the presentation is over. One by one, the audience members stand up and start to clap and cheer. Nelly looks over at Matthew and he simply gives her a thumbs up. That's all she needs to realise that she has done it!

The three of them come off the stage and are hugged by Benson and Amy.

"You were amazing Nelly. The best presentation ever!" screeches Amy.

Benson can barely speak because of his fat lip, but he still tries to smile! Dana squeezes Nelly's hand, "You saved the day Nelly, thank you," she gratefully tells her.

Nelly is grinning from ear to ear.

"I think the credit should go to UJ," she says. "Has anyone seen a better poster holder before?" With that, everyone laughs...or at least tries to laugh!

The presenter comes back on the stage.

“Ladies and gentlemen. Firstly, we must thank the four campaign presentations for their efforts. I can now proudly announce the winning campaign was presented by... the Bandu Club. Congratulations!”

The five of them jump up and down. Joe and Zane put Nelly on their shoulders, she fist pumps the air and the crowd goes wild!

Payback

‘Earn it, plant it, name it!’ is a huge success. A few hundred children turn up with their well-earned money and plant trees all over the empty field. Joe and Zane come along, plant a tree, and name it 'Nelly'. The local council are so impressed that they agree to find an empty field every year to carry on the Bandu Club's legacy.

***

After riding on a high, it's time for Nelly to get back to work. Her mum drops her off outside Matthew's office.

"Try your best!" she says.

"I always do!" replies Nelly.

She hasn't seen Matthew for a few weeks as she has been busy with the campaign and is looking forward to seeing him.

"Hi Nelly!" he says, opening the door to his room. They both sit down at the table. "The campaign was so much fun!" he continues.

"It was," says Nelly proudly.

"It was also a big success."

"It was," she says.

Where is he going with this? she wonders.

"It raised a lot of money."

"It did," she says.

Matthew laughs.

"The local council has agreed to use half of the money to buy trees for next year," he explains.

Nelly thinks for a moment, “What are they using the other half for?”

“Well...they were so impressed by you that they have donated the other half of the money to this centre, so that we can buy more resources and activities to help you and other children.”

Nelly can’t believe her ears!

“Really?” she asks.

“Yes really,” beams Matthew. “It’s what we call payback.”

Dana

Free as a bird

Dana helps lay the table whilst her dad puts the finishing touches to their lunch. Her dad is a chef and he always cooks amazing food. Today, he's whipped up her favourite...Borscht soup, made with beetroot, cabbage, and beef. He puts the soup bowls on the round table and they sit down together. Dana dunks her soft bread into her soup.

"So, what would you like to do this afternoon?" asks her dad.

"Can we go ice skating, please?" asks Dana, putting on her sweetest smile.

Her dad smiles, "Of course."

"Thanks, Dad. This is your best Borscht yet!" She always knows how to win her dad over!

After lunch, Dana and her dad jump into his car and they drive to the ice rink. Dana's heart is pounding with excitement and she can't wait to feel the cool air. When they arrive, Dana runs to the counter to check out the rows of boots. She stands admiring them and is really hoping for a silver pair. Hooray! They have her size in silver! Dana pulls on the heavy boots and stands up, wobbling just a little. Her dad pulls his on too and Dana offers him her hands to help him balance. They shuffle to the edge of the rink and both take a big step onto the ice. Her dad stays close to the edge and skates around slowly, using his arms to balance himself. After a few minutes of skating Dana feels her confidence rising. She glides around the rink and even does a few spins on the ice. She imagines wearing a silver glittered bodysuit to match her boots, whilst the audience admires her technique and gives her a round of applause. She forgets about everything going on in her life...she feels free as a bird.

This is Dana

Dana Petrova likes to wear her brown hair short. The style suits her face shape and on special occasions, she slicks it back with gel. She prefers wearing trousers and shorts, as she thinks dresses get in the way of adventure. Dana is ten and a half years old and her birthday is on the 5th of February. She is confident, independent, and likes to share her opinion.

Her dad is from Russia, which is why he likes to cook Borscht soup! She goes to Russian school on Sunday mornings; her dad says it's important to speak the language and be aware of her cultural heritage. Dana hasn't visited Russia yet, and her dad promises to take her when she's a teenager. Apparently, she has lots of aunts, uncles, and cousins there. For now, she is satisfied with imagining it with the help of books and the internet.

Dana is an only child. She likes it this way as she enjoys having friends around but then enjoys the quiet when they all leave. Her grandmother says she should appreciate it as she has her mum and dad all to herself. She wouldn't know – her grandmother has eleven brothers and sisters!

Dana can sometimes project a frosty exterior, with some kids assuming she doesn't like them. Since joining the Bandu Club, Benson has taught her to smile more; UJ has taught her to laugh out loud; Amy has shown her how to express herself through art and Nelly has taught her to communicate her feelings. She is grateful for the Bandu Club in more ways than one...and right now she really needs them.

Run

"Dana, can you please set the table?" asks her mum. Dana switches the TV off and puts the placemats and cutlery out. She walks into the kitchen.

"Can I help you with lunch?" she asks.

"No, it's ok. It's all ready," says her mum passing her a plate.

Dana looks down to see a cheese and tomato sandwich plus some cucumber strips on the side. *An OK lunch,* she thinks.

They sit down at the dining table to eat. "Dad made me Borscht soup the other day," says Dana.

"Oh, did he?" says her mum rolling her eyes.

This is her mum's signal that she doesn't want to talk about that subject.

"Do you think this dining table is too big? Your dad was the one who wanted a large table. I've never liked it. How about a smaller square one?" she asks Dana.

Dana who has little interest in dining tables, shrugs, and smiles at her mum, "Whatever you'd like, Mum."

After lunch, Dana goes upstairs as she has some Russian homework to finish before tomorrow. She flicks through her book whilst her music is playing in the background. She hears the doorbell ring; she hears her mum open the door; she then hears muffled voices. Leaning over she switches off the music and sits still to listen.

"I think she needs to stop Russian school as it's added pressure on her," her mum says.

"Stop Russian school? Are you mad? She enjoys it and it's so important for her. She is half Russian after all," snaps back her dad.

"Oh, and don't I know it, that's all I ever hear!" says her mum.

"You knew how important my heritage was to me before you married me."

"Well things have changed now, haven't they?" Her mum is becoming angrier with every reply.

Her parents are standing in the middle of the lounge facing each other. Dana can hear them discussing her grandmother, weekends, and school appointments. They raise their voices, and every time they do Dana feels sicker and sicker.

"I think you should leave!" she hears her mum say.

Dana can't stand listening to any more of this. She stands up and runs down the stairs. Ignoring them both, she slides on her trainers, slamming the door as she leaves. She runs down the street. Her mum follows her out of the house, shouting her name behind her, but she ignores her and keeps running.

Weird

That same afternoon Benson and Nelly meet up to play outside.

"Shall we go and knock for Dana?" Benson asks.

"Yeah, good idea," replies Nelly.

They walk in the direction of Dana's house. When they get to her house, they can see the lounge light is on, so Nelly rings the doorbell. They wait a while and then she rings again. Eventually, the door slowly opens and through the crack, they can see Dana's mum.

"Hi, can Dana come outside to play?" asks Benson.

"Erm, no sorry," answers her mum.

"Is she in? asks Nelly.

"Erm, no."

"Is she already out playing?" says Benson.

"Erm...she's busy...doing other things," mumbles her mum.

Benson and Nelly look at each other, sensing that she wants to close the door.

"Oh, ok," says Nelly. "We'll come round another day."

Dana's mum closes the door and they walk away in silence. After a few moments, Benson stops.

"That was weird," he says.

Nelly stops too and faces Benson.

"Yeah, it was. Dana's mum is normally so friendly."

"I wonder where Dana is," says Benson.

Both of them are worried and no longer feel like playing.

The best listener

Dana reaches Amy's apartment building. She has too much energy to use the lift, so she runs up the three flights of stairs.

"Please be in, please be in," she murmurs to herself.

She rings the doorbell and is relieved to hear footsteps. Amy's dad opens the door.

"Hi, is Amy in?" asks Dana, catching her breath.

“Come in, come in,” he ushers. “Amy, you have a visitor!” he shouts.

Amy flies around the corner and is happy to see Dana. She notices that Dana doesn’t look her usual self.

“Are you ok?” asks Amy.

“Not really.”

“Come on, let’s go to my room.”

Amy closes the door behind her. They both sit down on the bed and Dana starts sobbing into her hands. Amy puts her hand on Dana’s shoulder and waits patiently until she’s ready to talk. Dana slowly looks up at her with red puffy eyes.

“It’s the worst, Amy.”

“What is it, what’s happened?” asks Amy gently.

“My mum and dad have separated. My dad has moved out into his own apartment.”

"Oh my goodness. I can't believe that your dad has moved out. I had no idea."

"He moved out about three weeks ago. I've been spending time at his apartment."

"Has something happened today to upset you?" asks Amy.

"My dad came over to the house, and he and Mum started arguing. I couldn't take it any longer and that's why I came here. I just wish they could get along, but all they seem to do is argue."

Amy doesn't know anyone whose parents have split up, but she can see how heartbroken Dana is.

"Do you know why they split up?" she asks.

"Dad says that they still love each other, but are not in love with each other anymore. Mum has an angrier version," says Dana.

“I’m not sure I understand that. I’ll ask Mae later; I’m sure she will know.”

The two of them continue to talk and Amy even manages to get a few smiles out of Dana. Amy’s dad cooks them some noodles which they devour at the dining table. Back in the bedroom, Dana looks out of the window and notices that it’s getting dark.

“Perhaps I should go home...”

“Why don’t I ask Mae to walk with us?”

"Sure," says Dana.

The girls walk her back and they stand in front of Dana's house. Dana hugs Amy.

"Thanks for being the best listener."

"Anytime," replies Amy smiling.

"By the way Dana, your mum called so she knows you were at our place," says Mae.

"Ok, thanks for telling me."

Dana lifts up the blue flowerpot, finds the house key, and opens the door holding her breath. The house is dark and quiet. Dana flicks on the lounge light and sees a note on the coffee table.

I have gone to bed with a migraine. Sorry about earlier. Love Mum x

Dana gets herself a glass of water and walks up the stairs to her bedroom. She is exhausted and hopes tomorrow will be a better day.

As Amy and Mae walk home, Amy remembers that she has something to ask her.

"Dana's parents have separated," she tells her sister.

"I gathered something like that had happened. Poor Dana," says Mae.

"Dana said her parents still love each other but are not in love with each other anymore. What does that mean?"

Mae had heard this phrase on TV recently and was pretty sure she understood its meaning.

"I think her parents still have love for each other especially as they share Dana, but the feelings of being in love have gone. I guess they're not right for each other anymore," she explains.

"Love is complicated. I don't think I ever want to be in love," says Amy.

Mae laughs, "Love is grand Amy, believe me. You'll get there one day!"

She gives her sister a nudge and they both run the rest of the way home together.

Distraction

Dana wakes up feeling excited. Today the Bandu Club are going to the cinema and she is glad for the distraction. Her mum has been having mood swings recently—some days she is angry whilst on other days, she is quiet and barely talks. *I wonder what she'll be like today?* she thinks.

Dana helps make scrambled eggs on toast for breakfast. She loves cracking the eggs and beating them together. Her mum seems to be in a brighter mood.

"So what movie are you going to see?" asks her mum over breakfast.

"I can't remember the name of it, but it's about the adventures of a group of friends."

"Sounds like the Bandu Club," says her mum smiling.

Dana has thought about telling the Bandu Club about her parents and will see if the timing is right today. They all meet outside the cinema and Nelly's brother Zane has come along as a chaperone. He's happy to do so if he gets a Coke and popcorn! They sit in the back row to watch the movie, happily munching snacks and slurping drinks.

Afterwards, Zane takes them to a diner. They all pack into a booth and order milkshakes and burgers.

"So, what did everyone think of the movie?" asks Benson.

“My favourite part was when the monkey helped them escape from the zoo. Man, I would love to have a pet monkey,” says UJ.

“Firstly, that part about the zoo would never happen in real life, and secondly, it’s cruel to have a monkey as a pet,” says Nelly scowling at UJ.

“It’s just a movie!” UJ snaps back.

“Alright, alright,” says Benson. Before it can turn into a full-blown debate, the burgers and milkshakes arrive just in time to distract everyone.

As they are chomping away, Nelly brings up the movie again.

“I think the best part was when the girl, Marie, got her parents to talk to each other, she was so brave,” she says.

“Yeah, what was going on with her parents?” asks UJ, who has by now cooled down.

"They were getting a divorce," replies Benson.

"What's a divorce?" asks UJ.

"When a married couple decides not to be together anymore. My friend Corey's parents are divorced. Some days he lives with his mum and other times with his dad. He seems ok about it," says Benson.

"It must be hard though," says Nelly, who starts to well up with tears.

"But thankfully Marie's parents stopped arguing and that was all thanks to her," says Benson.

"It's just a movie," says UJ rolling his eyes, to which Nelly nudges him in the ribs.

Dana and Amy keep quiet throughout the conversation. Amy catches Dana's eye and gives her a smile. Dana smiles back and takes a sip of her milkshake. Her appetite has disappeared, and she leaves most of her burger uneaten.

Zane, who has been on his phone for most of their conversation, lifts his head.

“Alright guys, are we good to go?” he asks.

They pay up and leave. Dana is catching a lift home with Nelly and Zane. Their dad pulls up in his car and they get in. Sitting in the back together Nelly starts thinking about the other afternoon.

“Benson and I called around for you last Saturday. Your mum said you weren’t in and she seemed a little off.”

Dana’s mind races. She quickly plays back Saturday in her mind. *Oh yes! Argument...running...Amy.*

“Oh, I was out with my dad. My mum had a migraine and she’s a bit weird when that happens. But thanks for calling round.”

‘No worries, your poor mum,” replies Nelly.

For the rest of the journey, Dana is quiet and feels terrible for not being able to tell Nelly the truth.

She knows that one day she will, she's just not sure when. Although, there is one thing she is sure of...what her next step will be....

Marie saves the day

Dana returns home that afternoon and asks her mum if Dad can come over tomorrow morning.

"Really? But you have Russian school in the morning," says her mum.

"You now seem bothered about me going to Russian school?"

Her mum smiles and knows she's right.

"I'll send a message to your dad."

"Thanks," says Dana walking upstairs.

"I hope there's a good reason for this," her mum shouts after her.

Dana doesn't reply.

She spends the duration of her shower re-enacting the scene with Marie and her parents.

She really hopes her plan will work, as she wants to see her mum and dad happy again.

Her dad comes over at 10 o'clock the next morning and the first thing he mentions is the fact that Dana is missing Russian school! Before her mum can answer him, Dana asks them both to sit at the dining table. Dana has prepared large notepads and some marker pens.

"Ok, what I would like us to do is make a 'Same, Change and Work On chart'," Dana says.

Her mum is about to protest but stops herself when she sees how serious Dana is. Her parents listen as she describes the three headings. After sharing their thoughts, they decide what should be placed under each heading.

Same

We are a family

We love each other

We are there for each other

Dana continues with Russian school

Change

Mum and Dad live separately (Mum in Mable, Dad in the nearby town of Shirdie)

Dana will live in both homes

Work On

Listening to each other

Accepting each other's point of view

Being happy

Smiling and laughing more (this is Dana's suggestion)

Dana is really happy with the charts and suggests that they have copies in both homes. Her mum and dad agree. Dana is shocked, she hasn't seen them agree on anything in ages! Her parents both seem happier already as if a weight has been lifted. They even have lunch together and her mum makes more than a sandwich...they have omelettes!

The right time

Dana's mum suggests that Amy comes over to the house. Dana hasn't had friends over in a few weeks, so she takes this as a step forward.

Amy arrives with a tub full of warm dumplings. They give a plateful to Dana's mum, then go upstairs with the rest. They make themselves comfortable on Dana's bed. After catching up on school chat, Amy plucks up the courage to ask how things are with her parents.

"We made a 'Same, Change, and Work On' chart," says Dana smiling.

"Oh wow! Just like in the movie. Has it helped?" asks Amy.

"Yeah, it has. It's still early days, but my mum and dad already seem happier AND they haven't had an argument since."

"Well done Dana! I'm sure your parents are really proud of you."

"Thanks. Obviously, I would like them to get back together, but that movie made me realise that sometimes adults change, and life changes. I do want to tell the Bandu Club about my parents but at the moment I am happy that just you know. There will come a time—the right time, to tell the others. Just right now isn't it," says Dana.

Amy looks at her friend in admiration and realises just how brave Dana is. At that moment Dana's mum pops her head around the door.

"Those were the best dumplings I have ever had. Tell your dad he can make them for me anytime!"

They all laugh. Dana's mum sits down between them and takes out a couple of nail polish bottles from her jeans pocket.

"Pamper time!" she says, and the three of them get to work on each other's nails.

Dana's boudoir

As time goes by, Dana is starting to adjust to spending time at both her home and her dad's apartment. Dana has a beautifully decorated bedroom at home and her dad is conscious of this. At his apartment, she sleeps on a blow-up mattress. After a lovely Friday evening together, watching a movie and eating popcorn, he makes a suggestion.

"How about we go to Furniture Land tomorrow and buy some new things for your bedroom here?"

"That would be great!" replies Dana.

The next day after breakfast, they head to Furniture Land. Dana chooses a pretty pine bed; some patterned cushions and turquoise curtains; a bedside cabinet, and pictures of penguins to put on the wall. When they get back, her dad gets to work, and within a few hours, her new bedroom is ready. He has left Dana in the lounge and is ready for the reveal.

"Dana, it's ready!" he shouts. "Close your eyes," he tells her, leading her into the room.

"Ta-da...Dana's boudoir!" he says, proudly holding up his arms.

Dana opens her eyes and is blown away by how great her new room looks. She hugs her dad.

"Thanks, Dad, you're the best!"

"No Dana...you really are the best!"

He turns his head slightly so that Dana can't see the tears in his eyes, and he squeezes her a little tighter.

UJ

Christmas is coming

It is Saturday afternoon and UJ and his family are getting ready to meet their relatives for dinner at their favourite restaurant, Mario's. UJ is dressed in his blue cord trousers and a matching blue checked shirt; he looks very smart. They have been going to the restaurant for years and they know the owner well; his name is Mario (obviously!). It is a cosy Italian restaurant serving the best pizzas and pasta in town. There are red and white checked tablecloths, wine bottle candlesticks, and all the staff are Italian. UJ loves it there and his favourite dish is spaghetti with home-made pesto.

As they travel into town by car, UJ gazes out of the window. It's dark outside, the streetlights are on and he can see lots of people with shopping bags. They all look happy to be walking around wrapped up against the cold in winter coats. He spots tall fir trees decorated with lights, baubles, and tinsel. As they approach the town, he can see colourful strings of lights stretched across the high street and the restaurants are starting to fill up. They park the car and walk around the corner to Mario's. As they enter the restaurant, the sound of "Jingle Bells" softly plays in the background. *This can only mean one thing*, thinks UJ....*it's nearly Christmas!*

This is UJ

What UJ Abelman lacks in height he makes up for in energy. UJ is still waiting for his growth spurt and his dad reassures him he will be six foot three when he grows up. He has floppy light brown hair and is normally dressed in athletic clothes. UJ loves sports and he always picks them up quickly. He tried golf with his dad and shot a hole in one.

He's a strong swimmer and his nickname during lessons is "Fish." He's the fastest runner at school and the only sport which stumps him is basketball…he isn't quite tall enough to shoot the ball into the net! If UJ had enough time in the day, he would be practising with Benson constantly.

UJ has a lively family—mum, dad, and his twin sister Rosa. They live in a big house with an even bigger garden in Mable. The twins were born on the 2nd of September which makes them ten years old. His sister was born six minutes before UJ, of which she often reminds him, "I'm the oldest, so I should go first."

UJ is in fact a nickname. His actual name is Urijah John. His parents started calling him UJ when he was only a few months old and it has stuck. He likes to ask lots of questions. His mum has always told him to ask if he doesn't understand, and that's exactly what he does! He also likes to make people laugh and the more they laugh, the happier UJ is! He loves being part of the Bandu Club because of all the fun that they have, but also because there are girls in the club. He used to think girls were boring but as time goes by, Dana, Amy, and Nelly continually prove him wrong!

Mega

UJ's mum has been talking on the phone for ages.

"It's decided then, you can all come to us this year. We have lots of space."

She stops to listen to her sister.

"Why don't you bring dessert and we will make all the other food?"

She stops to listen again.

"Perfect, speak soon, bye," she says and puts her phone down.

UJ's mum looks around the lounge and sees that the whole family is all within earshot.

"Everyone is coming to us on Sunday the 20th. Please keep it free!"

"Ok," the rest of his family chime back.

"Oh, and we're going to Aunt Miriam's house on Sunday the 13th to start lighting the candles. Keep that free too!"

UJ, who is on the sofa watching a basketball game on TV, makes a mental note of the dates...although he's pretty sure he'll forget!

***

Dana really hopes that the Bandu Club can arrange a date to go to the theme park before Christmas. That was her suggestion when they all voted a few months ago and she's been patiently waiting despite her desperation to try the new rollercoaster. She heard that they put up Christmas decorations around the theme park, making it all the more exciting. She's going to suggest it tomorrow at their next meet up at Nelly's house.

***

Everyone turns up at Nelly's house enthusiastic as usual. They all sit around in her attic, lounging on the sofas. She helped her mum prepare hummus and vegetable sticks for snacks, and everyone dives in. Dana doesn't hold back and brings up her suggestion right away.

"What do we think about a trip to the Mega theme park? I still really want to try the new rollercoaster," she says.

Benson's eyes light up, remembering that he had voted for the theme park.

"I'm up for that!" he says, not dwelling on the fact that his basketball team idea had been voted out.

Amy is the most reluctant as she's pretty scared of fast rides.

"Once you are there and the adrenaline starts pumping, you won't be able to say no!" says Dana, trying her best to convince Amy. "My dad said that he would drive us all there," she adds.

"Cool!" says UJ, "which date are you thinking?"

"Well, the only date my dad can do so close to Christmas is Sunday the 13th," replies Dana. "I will have to miss my Russian class," she says with a twinkle in her eye.

"I will check with my mum, but I'm pretty sure that will be ok," says Nelly.

Amy and Benson say the same too. Whilst they are busy talking dates, UJ is unusually quiet. He knows that Sunday the 13th rings a bell with him. *Was it someone's birthday? Did he have to go somewhere?* Oh yes...he remembers! *Aunt Miriam's house!*

"Oh no, I can't go on that day," he says.

"Oh, why not?" asks Dana.

"I have to go to my Aunt Miriam's house."

"Can't you ask your parents to miss it?" asks Benson.

"Erm...no...I have to go," replies UJ.

"Why? Why is it so important?" asks Dana.

UJ starts to feel irritated, "I just do!"

The others take this as a cue to stop asking questions.

"You guys go ahead without me," says UJ flopping back onto the sofa.

Sunday 13th December

Sunday the 13th arrives and UJ has mixed emotions. He knows the rest of the Bandu Club are going to Mega to try out the new rollercoaster. He knows they will stop and eat French fries and popcorn. He knows that they will sing songs in the car. He knows that they will laugh and have a ton of fun. He knows that he is missing out. But, on the other hand, he knows that he will be spending the day with his family, and family comes first.

UJ and his family arrive at Aunt Miriam's house at lunchtime. They are all hungry and ready to eat. His dad has bought challah bread at the bakery to contribute to the lunch buffet. As they walk into the dining room the smells are amazing. They can see latkes (potato pancakes), blintzes (sweet pancakes), beef brisket, and matzo ball soup...it's a feast for the eyes! For dessert, there are sufganiyots (doughnuts), which are UJ's favourite.

After a long lunch, it starts to get dark outside. Everyone is feeling content, relaxing in the cosy lounge.

"Let's light the first candle," Aunt Miriam suggests.

All the aunts, uncles, and cousins crowd around the dining table and the youngest family member is allowed to light the first candle, and that's Cousin Immanuel. There are seven candles in total and UJ knows that he will get a turn to light a candle at home. The glow of the first candle reflects on everyone's faces and UJ feels happy.

UJ's family are Jewish and this is the beginning of their Hanukkah celebration. Hanukkah is the 'festival of lights' and is celebrated for eight days and nights. UJ knows that he has a lot more to learn about Hanukkah, but at this moment it represents family, food, and good times.

UJ has never told the rest of the Bandu Club that he's Jewish. He doesn't feel embarrassed, in fact, he's very proud of being Jewish. He just doesn't want to explain and answer all of the questions that will follow. His family doesn't celebrate Christmas and this is the one part of his religion that makes him feel different from his friends. He knows that in December they decorate their tree, receive lots of gifts, and eat turkey with all the trimmings. Since he has known the Bandu Club, his family would travel to Aunt Miriam's holiday home every 'Christmas' holiday. However, her husband, Uncle Alex, lost his job last year and because money is tight, they sold their holiday home, meaning that this year they are going to be home. UJ guesses that's how the question has never popped up because his friends always think he goes away for Christmas.

UJ and his family have a wonderful time at Aunt Miriam's. They leave with cartons of latkes and beef brisket. The drive home is quiet as Rosa and his mum fall asleep. UJ stays awake and daydreams about riding on the new rollercoaster.

Scream if you wanna go faster

Meanwhile, the rest of the Bandu Club are driven to Mega theme park by Dana's dad. They sing songs in the car on the way there and chat excitedly about the prospect of going on all of the rides.

When they arrive, they find a map of the park and devise a plan of where to go first.

“I think we just head straight to the new rollercoaster,” suggests Dana.

“Yeah, before it gets too busy and we have to wait for ages,” agrees Benson.

Ever since the camping adventure, Benson is now known as the ‘King of Directions’, so he leads the way. Luckily for them, the wait is only twenty minutes long, and that soon flies by. Dana pairs with Nelly, and Benson pairs with Amy. He promises to hold her hand if she becomes too scared! Dana’s dad is going to ride solo.

Dana is desperate to sit at the front of the rollercoaster, as she believes that will make it go faster. As they enter the final section of the line, they are all excitedly nervous.

Dana and Nelly step into the front carriage, whilst Benson and Amy sit behind them. The rollercoaster jolts, and slowly starts its journey up the first part of the track. They travel up high, and the higher they go, the more Amy wants to change her mind. As they reach the top, they all look out and enjoy the view. Before they know it...the rollercoaster builds up speed and zooms down the bending track. "Weeeeeeeeeee!!!!"

"Oh, my gooooodness!!!" screams Amy. She grabs Benson's hand, who himself is desperately trying not to scream!

Dana and Nelly are squealing with delight and hold their hands up as they whizz around the track. The rollercoaster approaches its first loop and Amy thinks she's going to faint! The rollercoaster turns upside down as it speeds around the circular track and Benson lets out an almighty, "Ahhhhhhhhhh!"

After a few more loops the ride comes to the end. As they come to a stop, everyone's hair is ruffled and most of them have big smiles on their faces. They all get out of the carriages on wobbly legs.

"Erm, I think I enjoyed that," says Amy, finding a bench to sit on.

"That was awesome!" says Benson.

As they chat about the ride, Dana realises she hasn't seen her dad. They wait by the bench and eventually her dad walks out looking very pale.

"Are you ok, Dad?" asks Dana.

Before he can answer, he puts his hand to his mouth and runs into the toilets.

"I guess your dad didn't enjoy the ride!" jokes Benson.

They all let out a little laugh and decide that they will let Dana's dad rest whilst they wait in line again...and again!

That evening Benson calls UJ.

“Ah man, the rollercoaster was epic! It went up so high and we looped the loop about five times. It was so good that we went on it three times in a row.”

UJ eagerly listens and imagines the rides as Benson describes them in detail.

“Did you eat French fries and popcorn?” UJ asks.

“Yeah, how do you know?”

“I know you guys too well!” laughs UJ.

“So, how was your day?” asks Benson.

“Yeah, it was good, thanks for asking. I ate so much that I still feel stuffed.”

“Was it somebody’s birthday?”

“Er...no,” replies UJ.

He thinks for a second.

"One day I'll explain it all to you," he says.

Benson is intrigued and says that he will see him soon.

Invitation

Over the next few days, UJ and his family light a candle at home. His parents allow UJ and Rosa to take turns. It's Wednesday night and whilst they are all relaxing in the lounge beside the glow of the candles, his dad comes up with a bright idea.

"UJ, why don't we invite the Bandu Club and their families to the party on Sunday?"

UJ looks startled.

"What do you think?" asks his dad.

"What a wonderful idea! The more the merrier," says his mum.

"That's a lot of people," UJ finally replies.

"We have enough space, plus it would be lovely for them to see how we celebrate Hanukkah," says his dad.

UJ knows that this would be the perfect opportunity to reveal his secret to his friends.

"Sure," he says smiling.

By Friday, his mum confirms that they are all coming to the party, apart from Dana's dad who will be traveling. UJ feels nervous, excited, and proud all at once. He knows he will need to prepare some answers and get ready for all of those questions!

Party!

The day of the party has arrived. UJ wakes up to a madhouse! Aunt Miriam is already there at 9 o'clock in the morning. His mum and aunt are frantically trying to cook every Jewish dish they can think of, as they are out to impress. UJ's dad is busy hoovering the whole house, and even Rosa has a duster in her hand.

"What can I do to help?" he asks after getting dressed.

His mum places a cloth in his hand.

"Please polish the cutlery and fold the napkins," she says.

Is the Queen coming? thinks UJ. There are fresh flowers in vases all over the house, and extra chairs have been placed around the lounge. Everyone is invited to lunch at 1 o'clock. The rest of UJ's family appear slightly before that, and even they are assigned jobs. Finally, the party is ready!

The first to arrive are Nelly and her parents, followed by Amy and Benson's families. Benson has also brought his sister Bianca who's eager to play with Rosa. The last to arrive is Dana who just comes along with her mum. UJ is relieved that his parents are happy to explain what Hanukkah involves, including the food and the lighting of the candles. The atmosphere is electric—with people chatting, eating, and learning about each other's cultures.

"Can we light the candle?" asks Rosa.

Everyone gathers around the dining table and a delighted Bianca lights the last candle. The candles are now all lit and look magnificent.

Later, the Bandu Club congregate in the conservatory at the back of the house.

"What a great party. My parents have asked your mum for the recipes, they love the food," says Amy.

"Nice!" replies UJ.

"It's cool that you are Jewish," says Benson.

"Yeah, I never really thought about telling you guys, but I'm glad you all know now. I guess we lead our lives a little bit differently," says UJ.

Benson is keen to learn more about his friend's religion.

"We've learned about Hanukkah today. What else can you tell us?" he asks UJ.

"If you think Hanukkah is fun wait till you come to my Bar Mitzvah. When I'm thirteen, I will have a ceremony and party to celebrate becoming a member of the Jewish community. I went to my cousin's Bar Mitzvah; it was so much fun with food and dancing. The only part which I'm nervous about is reading from the Torah."

"What's the Torah?" asks Nelly.

"Just think of it as the Bible. I'll go to classes to practise reading it, and then read out loud to everyone at my Bar Mitzvah," replies UJ.

"I can't wait for it, you'll be great," says Nelly.

Dana who has been quiet during the party clears her throat.

"It sounds amazing UJ. Erm...I have something to tell you guys," she says.

They all turn to look at her.

"My parents are getting divorced."

They are all quiet for a few moments. Amy who is sitting next to Dana reaches for her hand.

"I am really sorry to hear that," says Nelly.

"So am I," says Benson, who quickly thinks back to the time they knocked for Dana and they were met by her sad mum.

“It’s getting better now as Mum and Dad are talking more. You’ll have to come over to my dad’s apartment, he just decorated my bedroom,” she says.

‘Of course, we will!” says Amy.

UJ grins, “It really is the day for secrets.”

The Bandu Club smile, and for a few moments, they sit and reflect on their own secrets; the secrets that they have bravely shared with each other.

Mamma Mia!

UJ picks up the post and hands it to his mum. As she rifles through it, she notices a red envelope with fancy writing on it. She quickly opens it and gasps in excitement.

"Ooh, Mario has invited us to his restaurant on Christmas day for an Italian feast," she says.

Even though they have only ever spent the holidays with family, they all agree that a feast at Mario's will be the perfect alternative.

December the 25th arrives, and with the family dressed in their finest clothes, Mario welcomes them with open arms.

"Mamma mia, my favourite family!" he exclaims.

He gives them each a warm hug and sits them down at his best table. The restaurant is full of Mario's closest friends and family. Mario hands UJ and Rosa each a gift, all wrapped up in sparkly Christmas paper. Even though they typically don't exchange Christmas presents, UJ's parents encourage the children to open the presents and enjoy them. UJ is chuffed to receive a baseball cap and Rosa is over the moon with her Jenga game.

The family eats copious amounts of pizza, pasta, steak, and salad. At the end of the meal, Mario brings out a huge tiramisu and, "We Wish You a Merry Christmas", plays out of the speakers as he walks in.

UJ looks at Mario; he looks at all of the people singing, and he looks at his family. He feels proud and grateful for his wonderful life. He cannot wait for the New Year and for more exciting adventures with the Bandu Club!

THE END

Carla Campbell

I loved to write poetry and stories growing up in the UK. Then life got in the way and I had a ball...university; work; travel; moving to Hong Kong; becoming a teacher; marrying the man of my dreams; travelling some more; becoming a mother and a move to Amsterdam. I then found myself with time on my hands...and I decided to write. It has been an amazing process of learning, persistence and confidence building...to finally...The Bandu Club being born! I think every child should read this book; friendship, acceptance and diversity are so important in the world right now. I hope the story puts a smile on your face and lets you reach out to a friend.

Ryan Hummer

I am a teacher, artist, outdoor enthusiast and creator of the Hong Kong Coloring Book. I grew up in Seattle, USA and have resided in Hong Kong since 2005. I love sharing my passion for art with my students, family and anyone else who appreciates beauty. I hope you enjoy the illustrations in The Bandu Club and follow your passions wherever they may take you.

Thank You

Thank you to Aidan and Thia for being my world. A huge thank you to my good friend Ryan who illustrated the book. His artistic ability and loyalty to the project blew me away. Thanks to my brother Ian who read my initial manuscript and gave me his first ever compliment after 42 years! Endless thanks to my sister Nic, who has always championed everything I do. Thanks to Antony, who listened, listened and listened some more and instilled a greater confidence in me. A big shout out to my eclectic, colourful friends all over the world, who have stuck by me through thick and thin. You are my Bandu Club!

Thank you to the professionals – beta readers, editors, and designers who helped me turn my pipe dream into reality. Thanks to the author Mat Waugh who took time to answer my questions and provided me with invaluable insight.

Thank you to Iris and Norman who brought me into this world, who left me too soon, yet taught me to reach for the stars. Dad...I typed out every word of this book on your PC!

Carla x

Printed in Great Britain
by Amazon

28220062R00091